Evolutionarium

Air

By Andrea Mina Savar

"Be like the bird who, pausing in her flight awhile on boughs too slight, feels them give way beneath her, and yet sings, knowing she hath wings."

-Victor Hugo

Jasper was a collector of tiny things. His first memories were not of parental doting but rather the glimmer of treasures submerged in sand. An ocean-smoothed shard of glass or an acorn freshly fallen to block his path. These were the things that captured his blue eye. At first his mother had cooed that he was a genius among children. Her arms made a gentle flapping noise as she lifted her hands in expressive joy while proclaiming the virtues of her attentive son. But by his tenth birthday, the praise turned into a violent caw.

"Exasperating! You are. Why must you waste time on meaningless things?" she would squawk as he stopped to observe a snail. A leaf covered in dew. A spider spinning its web. A dotted stripe on a napkin. Jasper's father understood him even less. His appraising looks were often tinged with a hint of regret. A child so unlike himself seemed unnatural. He pondered why his son preoccupied himself with oddities of nature. The courtyard of their apartment complex filled each evening with the playful shouts of boys engaging in various ball games. A quick glance outside provided him with nightly disappointment. His spectacled eyes fell upon the flock of children playing with delight. A small flutter of hope to see his son amongst them was always extinguished when he spied Jasper perched in his usual spot. Tonight it was a white feather that had the boy transfixed. His legs folded neatly on the blue park bench.

To Jasper these tiny worlds were far from mundane. In each sparkling fragment of the miniscule, he saw a puzzle piece of the universe. It was a way for him to make sense of a much larger, more cumbersome existence. A way to possibly understand the evolution he sensed was underway. He watched as night moths fought their way free of cocoons. They struggled towards the air, moved by the instinct of metamorphosis, to expand speckled wings on windowpanes.

His neighbor, Mrs. Harlow, liked to capture them in jars. She had shown Jasper how to mount and frame the tiny beasts. The walls of her abode were lined with immortalized creatures. When his family had moved into the complex on the hill a few months earlier, she had been the first person to greet them. A plate of dry cookies and a cracked teapot sat in the midst of specimens innumerable. The crack in the teapot reminded Jasper of the cracks in the cement walls outside.

The tower of doors and windows stacked on top of each other created a dismal habitation. Outside the bottom floor were chicken coops lined in zigzags that followed the grey pillars and beams of the apartment building. Mrs. Harlow lived on the seventh floor. Jasper hoped it was a lucky thing to live on seven, even if the structure itself was crumbling under the weight of overpopulation. He also wondered why everyone crowded and clucked over new openings when the top floor was entirely vacant.

"Old detritus and black mold, no place for children." This was what Mrs. Harlow had whispered when he inquired about the blocked stairwell to the top floor of the building. Piles of broken chair legs and drawer-less armoires created a dam, impassable. Jasper had ventured to explore all the nooks and crannies of their new home when they first arrived. He found a marble stuck where the old elevator button used to be. The lifts hadn't worked in decades so Jasper felt he was saving the shiny red orb from oblivion by prying it out of the ancient clasp. Each floor unveiled a forgotten treasure. An old postcard. A long forgotten key. A pearl-colored button. All of these he secreted away, even though they were a far cry from the treasures he found when they had lived by the ocean. Still, these trinkets would keep him company in a way nothing else could.

But the top floor remained a mystery. When he first laid eyes on the cacophony of broken furniture, it had reminded him of something. A woven nest of twigs he once found at the base of an ancient tree. He perceived it as organic in its construction, or destruction, depending on how one interpreted it. Jasper felt compelled to climb the uneven steps of the dark hallways each night before going in for dinner. He passed lucky seven and kept climbing until he faced the mountainous pile of metal and wood debris. It was the same each night.

Tonight Jasper spotted his father's outline against the window. A flash of light from the fading sun caught his spectacles giving an owlish quality to his scorn. Jasper had been examining a feather for the better part of the hour. Each wisp reminded him of something he couldn't quite recall. A link to a far off memory he hoped to unlock through further examination. Something he could never hope to explain to his perplexed father. In the feather, there was an escape from the high pitched wailing of his mother.

A shrill whistle from the upper windows signaled the children to come inside. The earth was moving away from the sun more rapidly these days. Jasper lingered for a moment after all the other children had bustled indoors. That was when he saw a shadow stir on the roof. A winged illusion? He wondered if his eyes were playing tricks on him. He had one brown eye and one blue. The latter spotted the sparkling things. The former sometimes perceived mysteries unmentionable. He felt a rush of fear shudder through his thin body. The courtyard was silent and the sky was a deepening violet. He ran past the coops and through the steel doors that led to his nightly shelter.

Heart thumping rapidly, he leaned against the entrance, fearful the winged shadow would follow him inside. Tonight, he went straight to floor seven and avoided the odd nest.

Jasper stood in front of his apartment door, fixed to one spot, dreading the noise inside. Were they arguing or talking? Sometimes he couldn't decipher the two, the volume tended to be the same. The words were only slightly different. Fidgeting with the feather, he turned and shuffled to the door a few paces to his right. Before he could knock, it creaked open.

Mrs. Harlow was ageless. There were mornings when Jasper spotted her rushing into the communal pea patch with a youthful blush. A woman younger than his mother, he wondered? Other times, when she made him tea, he noticed her hands had arthritic knots that twisted painfully like tortured branches. This evening, she raised a curious eyebrow with childlike wonder.

Her eyes flickered from him to the noise coming from his apartment. The walls were no more than thin slices of paper, haphazardly erected to give an illusion of privacy. She held the door open to Jasper, offering a moment of tranquility. He zipped inside, in case she suddenly changed her mind.

"Isn't it your dinner time?" she asked, as he seated himself in his usual chair. Mrs. Harlow had a small table for two under a vast window.

He liked to look at the city from this vantage. The lights, the last wisps of visible smoke before the night became black. Jasper also liked to check that his bench was still in the same place. Sometimes he imagined it shaking its legs free from the pavement to walk into the forest at night; a blue beast of sculpted metal. As long as it came back by morning, he didn't mind.

"I guess," he replied, cautiously scanning for winged shadows in the courtyard. Mrs. Harlow gave a merry tweet of acknowledgement.

"I won't give you cookies then," she said while shuffling though her cupboards. Jasper didn't care for dry cookies. All he wanted was a quiet place. He felt calm here; wanted. Mrs. Harlow settled in the chair opposite while placing a small plate conspiratorially between them. "Maybe a little snack won't hurt."

Instead of old cookies, there was something far more delectable. Jasper smiled wide at the fried crickets beautifully arranged on white porcelain. Mrs. Harlow pinched one between her tired fingers and popped the crispy treat in her mouth, motioning for him to do the same. He examined them quickly, perfect folded legs, sea salt, a slight sheen of oil. The one in the center of the plate was his first victim. When he plucked it from the dish, a four leaf clover appeared beneath it. A small detail of the plate exposed. Lucky clover, lucky seven, he thought. The texture was crunchy like fresh crackers; the taste was earthy like a long forgotten home.

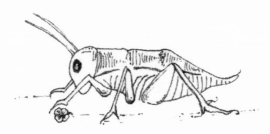

"Have you ever been to the top floor?" Jasper asked. His mind preoccupied with the form he had spied on the roof. Mrs. Harlow twisted a bit in her chair before glancing wistfully outside.

"A long time ago," she said softly. "Mr. Harlow liked to imagine we would move up there someday." He often wondered where Mr.

Harlow had gone. Grown-ups hushed him when he had asked. His bedroom shared a wall with Mrs. Harlow's apartment. Sometimes, very late at night, he thought he heard a man's voice whispering on the other side.

"What's it like up there?" he asked while snatching another plump cricket from the plate.

"It was magnificent," she smiled at Jasper; a youthful twinkle suddenly replaced the sadness in her sharp eyes. "Part of the roof is glass because there were gardens up there. The plants were nothing but dried stalks when I saw them. Now I imagine it's a tragic ruin. It was one, large habitation; a place where the wealthy once lived. Before the Great Change started."

He nodded, imagining the grandness of what had been. Again, Jasper wondered why no one lived there now. The apartments below overflowed with people contented to live in cages. It seemed odd not to put such a space to use. Then the image of the furniture nest came to mind. Was it built from the inside out or the outside in? Maybe something already lived there after all.

"Where is Mr. Harlow?" Jasper asked, rushing the words before he could talk himself out of speaking them. Mrs. Harlow slipped the last cricket inside her mouth. She ate it slowly while examining the darkness outside, chewing her words before speaking them. When she finished, she looked at Jasper with an odd tilt of her head. A crow-like gesture he had become accustomed to when speaking with Mrs. Harlow. It was her prefix when asked to respond to a question. Just as her lips parted, a raucous knock rattled the thin door to the apartment.

Jasper's stomach rolled with disappointment. Both at not having his question answered as well as by the certitude his father was on the other side of the door. As Mrs. Harlow crossed the room, Jasper spied something curious. There were two protrusions on either side of her thin shoulders. Her hair was twisted into a loose bun, exposing the delicate curve of her neck. One of her hands turned the doorknob; the other pulled the thin twig from her hair. Her dark locks cascaded free, obscuring the oddity. But not before Jasper glimpsed the rustle of a feather from beneath the back of her shirt.

Jasper slept in fits and starts. He had the one bedroom in the apartment to himself. His parents slept in the main room amidst jingly pots and pans. There was a string of laundry perpetually stretched from kitchen to couch. The stripes, dots and floral patterns were a loud banner of the quotidian. The sight of it made Jasper tired. He preferred more subdued colors; the kind that let him blend in against concrete walls and wood banisters.

He wasn't sure if he was given his own room out of generosity. It seemed more likely it was out of pity. Or worse, to tuck him out of sight. Regardless, it was starkly furnished with a small bed, wooden desk and chair, one window. Just the way he liked it.

A baby wailed, impossible to tame, in the room upstairs. A few floors below a violin whined a mournful tune. Laughs echoed in the hallway in synch with his parents chuckling and clinking glasses. But the other side of the wall was silent. From his window he perceived a subtle glow of candlelight from Mrs. Harlow's apartment. He wondered if she was luring moths to a divine death.

An intriguing hush resounded from the living room. This was

unusual considering there was a gaggle of his parents' friends gathered. Jasper could smell the vinegary aroma of apple beer through the closed door. His father worked in the orchards which meant a stipend of apples to ferment was gifted to them each year. Jasper was convinced if he ever drank the concoction it would shrivel his insides like salt on a slug. His parents assured him he would one day think otherwise.

But tonight, the hush surely meant someone was telling a secret. Jasper tiptoed out of bed and carefully cracked the door. It was opened a sliver, just enough to hear words obscured. He squatted on the floor, feet cold on the ancient tiles, and leaned in to spy. Just as he'd hoped, Mrs. Cygnus from the fourth floor held the group enraptured with moist gossip.

"Another one disappeared," she hissed and the group let out a muffled gasp. "Mr. Pava from floor nine, this time it was! He went in as usual last night but this morning he was gone! The door was locked from the inside. All his things were perfectly in place. An open window was all."

"He must have flown the coup," jeered Mr. Larus from floor five. The rest of the group gave a nervous laugh.

"Very curious indeed," his father sounded skeptical. There was a part of him that found gossip distasteful. His mother often maneuvered the words enough to sound like legitimate news so as not to offend his senses.

"That makes five in less than six months!" Mrs. Cygnus was keeping her hysteria to a raspy whisper. Jasper could smell her fear from across the room, a hint of bitter almonds.

"I don't mean to sound crass," his mother cooed coquettishly, "but that *is* how we ended up with this apartment, after all."

"Oh yes! Mr. Gryphus lived here...odd duck, really," Mr. Cygnus added. "He always kept to himself. Read books all the time. Some said he even wrote on paper, like they did before the Great Change. Put on airs, if you ask me."

"It was the same thing, poof!" Mrs. Larus replied. "Gone during the night like the others."

"The first was Mr. Harlow, of course," Mrs. Cygnus said while scrunching up the side of her face, one thumb pointed to the wall shared with Mrs. Harlow's apartment. "Talk about a strange character. Dashing, of course, but mad as a hatter."

"He talked rubbish about building a terrarium on the roof out of the old debris," Mr. Larus gave a cackle of condescension. "Never worked a day in the orchard, like the rest of us. Always dreaming, that one. He even drew his musings in chalk on the old walls of the boiler room. Utter madness!"

"Mrs. Harlow is better off, if you asked me," chimed Mrs. Larus. "But it's the little ones gone that have me worried. It's not natural for children to disappear like that."

Mrs. Larus' words floated in the room, leaving nervous silence in their path. Jasper heard his father give a cough before offering more apple beer. Soon the conversation shifted to talk of the bee trade. Jasper gently closed the door and walked to his bed. He had much to ponder.

There had been talk amongst the children in the courtyard about two of their ilk vanishing. Of course, Jasper had given the ravings little mind. He was more interested in how a dragonfly carcass could dry, unscathed. Or how his treasures were organized in the old tin he kept in his pocket. Now he wished he had paid more attention to what was being said.

Wrapped in his favorite cotton blanket, he closed his eyes and began to count the number of trees that lined the hill, from memory. It soothed him, focused the spinning sensation that chatter caused in his brain. After one hundred and twenty three, he drifted to sleep.

That night Jasper dreamt he was walking in a chalk maze drawn on the concrete courtyard. The winged shadow watched him, perched high on the rooftop, in the same manner that a falcon observes a field mouse.

There was an art to feigning illness. Jasper mastered the right combination of indiscriminate symptoms in order to stay home. Illness was taken seriously; one sick child could domino into a building cloistered in misery. His parents forbade him to leave his room while they were in the orchard. He watched from the window as children marched, in a neat row, behind their school master. Mr. Corvid led the little ducks to the learning shed, to memorize the laws of apples.

Jasper climbed back into bed. He fished his tin of treasures from beneath his pillow. It calmed him to line the elements into a pristine row. Old postcard, iron key, shell button, red marble, white feather; aligned perfectly. If he could make order of these pieces then maybe he could decipher the influx of elements from last night. Roof shadow, shoulder feather, missing neighbors, Mr. Harlow, chalk writing; violent disarray.

But nothing emerged. He tried to look at it sideways by tilting his head until he nearly fell off the bed. Still nothing. He stood up and looked down at the treasures from his full height, hoping to intimidate an answer. Silence. Giving up, he placed the objects carefully inside their tin resting place. Jasper took care to cradle each item first, so it knew he loved it.

His real reason for faking contagion was a longing desire to find Mr. Harlow's chalk drawings. It was the one part of the building he had yet to explore. Jasper had been avoiding it up until now. As much as he loved wandering the many hallways, the abandoned boiler room was a dark place. Each floor above ground housed a window in the stairwell and one at the end of each hall. Not the boiler room. Below ground there was nothing but blackness and damp. No place for children.

First, he dressed. Pajamas were not appropriate boiler room prowling wear. He tucked his tin of charms into his jacket pocket, feeling confident they would help protect him. Jasper took one of the beeswax candles from the drawer in the kitchen along with the bedtime candlestick holder. He knew better than to take more than one match. One could be overlooked; two might tip off his parents.

Steeling his nerve, Jasper made his way down the seven long flights. The building was silent. Everyone was either infirm, with the smaller children indoors, in the orchards or at the learning shed. He heard chickens clucking casually when he reached the main floor. It had been raining all morning and they were tucked inside the coops.

The door to the boiler room was nothing exceptional. A steel door, grey metal chipped and a rectangular mark where a plaque once announced the room's purpose. He swallowed his fear and twisted the abandoned handle. It took three tries before he could tug it open. The hinges were rusty with neglect. A quick grazing of his one match on the striker and the candle was aglow.

The stairs were a latticework of metal, only a dozen footfalls until he reached bottom. The room was small and held a tangle of pipes. The boiler was a massive contraption, silent after too many years of unappreciated servitude. It was a relic of another time when heat was taken for granted. Jasper ignored the obvious components of the room. He wanted to find the incongruous.

A melancholy drip plunked in the far corner. He followed it and was rewarded with the magnificent specter of Mr. Harlow's white chalk words. Floor to ceiling, overflowing hieroglyphs expanded into a mysterious mosaic. At first, Jasper tried to look at it close-up, nose nearly touching the delicate etchings. He had to keep the candle held aloft by his side, careful not to singe his hair. He had been clumsy on other occasions.

Numbers, letters, drawings of things innumerable; it was a mystery. Jasper stepped back from the wall, leaving the candle beneath it, to see the creation as a whole. Still it remained an enigma. Eventually he sat on the floor and began to memorize each puzzle piece. He counted on his fingers, recording lines in his mind, tapping his foot in unison. A metronome of memory. In this manner he sat, trance-like, oblivious that time would eclipse the candle.

When the flame flickered, Jasper knew it was too late. He had forgotten the hours, intent on understanding Mr. Harlow's secrets. The light stuttered then gave a resounding sigh of darkness. Alone in the boiler room, he heard the plunking of water and the occasional zip of a rat nearby. He inched forward until he found the useless candlestick. Then he closed his eyes, blind in the absence of light and began to walk by memory back to the stairs.

The plunk of water became distant, 29 paces then his shin found the first metal step. One dozen footfalls up, eyes closed, Jasper wondered if there were ghosts following silently behind him. Waiting until he pushed open the door to trap him forever. Remembering the rust, he leaned hard on the steel door, controlling his urge to flee. The creak of the hinges roared with joy, his eyelids flew open to the blinding light of the first floor.

A slight disorientation was soon replaced with crushing dread. Jasper had escaped the clutches of boiler room ghosts only to come nose to nose with his parents. The flood of residents returning from the orchards had coincided with his candle's demise. Caught, obviously not ill, and holding a stolen candle; Jasper knew the punishment would be severe.

His father didn't have to say a word. His mother tugged his arm and half dragged him to floor seven. These things were handled behind paper thin walls for the sake of propriety. Jasper's father tore the candlestick from his hands once inside their apartment. He had been clutching it like a safety blanket. The sound of children playing in the hallway punctuated the fact that their child was different. A slap in the face, his mother cried. Disappointed, his father bellowed.

The noise of their disapproval was punishment enough for Jasper. It pierced into all the sensitive points in his skull. Burrowing into the places where he stored the numbers and unraveled the coded mysteries of the universe. If only they had known how painful it all was for him, his mother never would have done the unthinkable. His passivity enraged her. His father watched over the top of his spectacles, reflecting that his child was a creature ill-equipped for survival. Each word-lash from his mother made Jasper retreat farther into himself. The final blow, the *coup de grace*, was when she tore his tin of treasures from his jacket pocket.

"You waste your time with idiotic trinkets," she wailed. "No more!" And with one violent gesture, she opened the window and threw his wingless tin from floor seven. He rushed to the window in a fit of futility to witness its descent. It curved through the air in an arch and then plummeted to the ground. The impact dissected the lid from the body. The precious contents were strewn to the four corners of the courtyard. He tried to memorize where they had gone. The old postcard caught in the wind, the iron key on a patch of weeds, the shell button in a puddle, the red marble under his bench, the feather in a concrete fissure. Broken, scattered, lost; these were his hopes, comforts, dreams.

Jasper went to bed without dinner. His eyes wide open, heart cracked like Mrs. Harlow's teapot.

Some children would have cried themselves to sleep. Not Jasper. He waited until the familiar sound of snoring resounded from the living room. He was still wearing his prowling clothes from earlier in the day. Cracking the door, he swiftly glided across the main room, shoes in hand. The clothesline wafted gently with the rhythms of his parents' nocturnal harrumphing.

In a flash, he was in the hallway. Tonight the moon was at its highest point, giving light to the otherwise dark corridors. Stealthily, Jasper moved with a determined pace, taking two steps at a time. He was on a rescue mission. The only moment he stopped to pause was when he reached the metal doors. Jasper had never been outside after nightfall. In fact, he couldn't remember anyone lingering in the courtyard when the moon was high. He thought of the roof shadow.

Jasper rested his hand on the door knob, his brain battling a silent tug of war between fear and compulsion. The minutes ticked away, stop clock clicking in his mind, until compulsion won. It always did with Jasper. His mother called him stubborn but it was more than a mere character flaw. Jasper's mind whirred, perpetually in motion, fixated on finding ethereal connections. When it stuck on an element, it refused to relinquish it. Even the most fleeting of notions became part of the movement. Friction was simply unacceptable to Jasper.

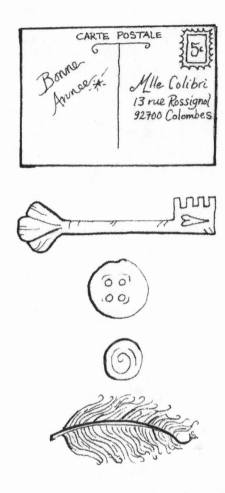

With a deep breath of courage, he pushed the metal door open and stepped into the abandoned courtyard. Silence. The day birds were tucked into their roosts, pillows fluffed, enjoying slumber. A profusion of puddles dotted the concrete; Jasper knew exactly which one held his shell button. First he gathered the two halves of his tin. Maybe a bit of string could hold it together, he thought. The top had been dented from the seven story swan dive.

The postcard had somersaulted to the far side of the concrete expanse where the hill began its decline towards the city. Jasper ran to where he thought he had seen it fall. The night sky was aglow with clusters of stars. The candle flickers from the city below were only a minor companion in luminosity. Damp with humidity, Jasper retrieved the limp piece of paper. The address was smeared; the stamp lifted on one edge. He slipped it into his pocket along with the tin. The iron key was only a few steps away. Now it was safe in his pocket as well.

Jasper scurried quickly to the puddle, reaching into the dark water without hesitation. A wriggling earth worm was his first discovery. He set it gently on the concrete where it could inch its way towards a patch of errant grass. Again, his hand dove into the murky puddle. He felt the curve of the shell button, instantly a flutter of relief thumped in his chest. It joined its old companions in his pocket.

In a flash, he was at the far end of the courtyard where he got on all fours under the blue bench. He knew the red marble was hiding under it. The indigo tinge of night made it more difficult to find. Inch by inch, he ran his palm along the pavement. Nothing. He moved behind the bench in case it had rolled. Still nothing. He sat back on his heels and felt an odd lump under his left shoe. Eureka! The red marble was home again.

Just as Jasper was about to stand, he felt a cool shiver run down his spine. Silence transformed into dead stillness. A shadow crossed the moon. He crouched behind the bars of the blue bench, a shudder of fear rushing through his limbs. He was not alone. Scanning the courtyard, nothing stirred. Jasper was afraid to look up but again compulsion tugged at his chin.

This time, instead of a shadow, he saw the complete figure of a winged man. It was emerging from the seventh floor window that belonged to his beloved neighbor. A lark-like shriek pierced the air as Mrs. Harlow was dragged by the shadow from her home. Legs dangling in mid-air, she lost consciousness. The creature hoisted her limp body under one arm as it scaled the building with ease.

Up past seven, eight, nine to the roof. Clawed feet catching on the fissures, one hand to anchor the weight. Its massive dark wings barely fluttered. Jasper gasped as the winged man, chest bared, stood on the building's edge. Mrs. Harlow draped at his side in a shocked stupor. The creature whipped its head, hawk-like, towards Jasper's exhalation of surprise. In that brief moment, he spied the winged creature's profile. Where a man's face should have been, there was instead a bird's countenance. Curved beak, sharp eyes, smoothed scalp of feathers leading to muscular human shoulders.

Jasper held his breath and did his best to blend into the concrete behind the bench. The bird-man scanned the courtyard slowly. His eyes stopped when they reached Jasper's hiding spot. The boy could feel the cold, hawk-eyes deciphering the shapes and shadows around him. A second longer and he would be discovered.

Even in unconsciousness, Mrs. Harlow came to Jasper's aid. A groan of fear escaped her lips, directing the bird-man's attention back to his captive. The shadow lifted Mrs. Harlow into its arms and disappeared into the glass structure on the roof. For the first time in Jasper's life, fear overtook compulsion. He ran to the metal door in a manic dash. He left the white feather behind.

By morning, Jasper's body was wracked with fever. His parents stood at his bedside, aware that this time their son was not inventing illness. Forehead on fire, chills racing through his limbs, he shook uncontrollably. Jasper floated between his bed and the nightmare he had witnessed in the courtyard. Was it a dream, he wondered? No. He could feel the comforting lump, his talisman tin, hidden under the mattress. Also, Mrs. Harlow's wall was abnormally silent. But then the improbability of the man-bird sent Jasper reeling into feverish delusion.

His parents had no choice but to leave him again for the day. It was picking time in the orchard; no one was exempt from work. With a slight tremor of regret, they left the frail boy with a pitcher of water by his bedside. He spent the morning restless, in and out of nightmares. By noon, he was able to consume the water. Jasper drank clumsily, letting the elixir cool his insides. In the afternoon, the fever broke and in its place were two burning spots on both shoulder blades.

Again he thought of Mrs. Harlow, the hint of feathers on her back. Jasper sat for a moment in bed, staring at his naked feet. The sun was starting to fade again, his parents would soon return. Slowly, he dressed, this time with methodical, energy-saving movements. One sock, foot thumped on the floor, then the other. The laces of his shoes squiggled like unwilling serpents. Finally he slipped his jacket on, the mangled talisman tin again in its rightful place; the right-side pocket.

When he arrived at the stairwell, he could hear the chatter of people flooding in from the main door, beginning their ascent home. Climbing, hand on the banister, Jasper moved upwards towards the mysterious roof. It had been over a day since he'd visited the furniture nest. He now knew what was on the other side, the man-bird. More so, Mrs. Harlow.

It took Jasper longer than usual to arrive at the top of the stairwell. His legs were rickety from fatigue. A few dusty crackers had been his only sustenance since noon. When he arrived at the final step, before the way became impassable, he crumbled to the floor. Knees pulled up to his chest, cheek against the cool tiles, he observed the nest sideways. It was identical, nothing out of place, which gave him a glimmer of pleasure.

Jasper had memorized every precarious angle in the peculiar arrangement from an upright position. It was a tangle of chaotic wooden arms and metal legs. But from the horizontal, he saw something he had never noticed before; a way in. Carefully, he crawled, on hands and knees, into the nest. The construction made perfect sense once he was inside. It went as follows: lift knee over wooden leg. Duck past mattress springs. Scoot sideways with back to the overturned desk. Shimmy through a tumble of chairs. In this manner he wove through the maze of debris and emerged on the other side.

Even at crepuscule, the roof breathed with odd light. Jasper stood at the opening of the glass house. He took every detail in, eyes hungrily filtering the information of the space. A ledge ran the edge of the building. The glass house was tucked neatly inside in precise alignment, a metal encasement held it aloft. In the center of the house was a terrarium stocked with long dead plants. The dry husks had once been trees at their tallest, now parched limbs unsalvageable.

Buckets lined one edge of the outside ledge, water collectors, much like what was used in the gardens below. Jasper's head buzzed with the aftermath of fever and the influx of information. He stepped silently inside, eyes alert to shadows, of which there were none. As he moved past abandoned furniture and impossible appliances, Jasper heard the faint creak of movement.

Stealthily, he rounded the edge of the terrarium. The source of the noise, a circular bed lined with pillows, suspended from a metal beam by a bramble of ropes. Inside of it, laid Mrs. Harlow. She appeared asleep, under a patchwork of blankets. Jasper noticed the sleeve of her housedress peeking from beneath the covers. It trembled delicately with each intake of breath.

Jasper felt a sun of relief ignite in his chest knowing she was alive. He moved to the edge of the bed and put his index finger on her shoulder. It was enough to stir Mrs. Harlow from sleep. At first, she stared at him blankly, eyes still misty with dream clouds. Then they burst wide with fear.

"Jasper," she hissed, "how did you get up here?"

"I climbed the stairs and went through the nest," he replied in a whisper.

"You can't be here," She said with a tremble. Mrs. Harlow tossed the blankets aside and carefully emerged from the suspended cocoon. Her dress slightly askew, feet bare as Jasper's had been.

"But I needed to find you," he mumbled, still unsure of the origin of his obsession with the furniture nest and what lay beyond.

Mrs. Harlow clutched his small hand in her own. With a determined tug, she pulled him back towards the stairwell. Then, as quickly as she had started, she stopped with a sudden jerk and turned to face Jasper. Head tilted in her curious crow manner, she placed her palm on his feverish forehead. The unwanted heat was back.

"When did the fever start?" she whispered, leaning down, her cheek grazing his own as the words tumbled into his left ear.

"Last night," he chocked, "after I saw the man-bird steal you." She nodded and moved behind him, lifting the back of his shirt.

"Does it burn here?" she asked, moving her cool fingers over the two spots on each shoulder that screamed with heat. He nodded an affirmation.

"Don't be afraid," she hummed, "it only hurts at first; then the wings will break though." Jasper nodded only vaguely comprehending. Instead of pulling him towards the stairwell, she led him back to the cocoon bed. This time Mrs. Harlow helped him into the indention where she had been only moments before. He could smell her familiar perfume on the pillows; lilacs and autumn rain. She tucked him in tight with blankets.

Jasper saw two things before fever and exhaustion overtook him in sleep. The first was Mrs. Harlow glide to the far side of the glass house. She walked with purpose towards the two doors that opened to the ledge. There the bird-man's silhouette stood observing the world below. The second was a small pile of bones stacked haphazardly in the corner. Tangled within them were two pairs of children's shoes.

Mr. Harlow had always suspected he was slightly different than the rest of the flock. Keen observation alerted him that the Great Change was only in its first stages. People were getting comfortable in the new normal. Not Mr. Harlow, he scanned the horizon, survival instincts alive in his limbs. At first, his wife Maggie tried to comfort him, worrying he would make himself ill. Late nights in the boiler room, writing on walls, was the only thing that kept his mind from spiraling downwards.

The night the fever struck, Maggie's concern shifted to solemn understanding. When the wings burst forth, he felt a combination of terror and relief. Terror in the physical implications yet relief he had not imagined it all in madness. That was when he barricaded himself on the rooftop. The next evolution would not go unnoticed by neighbors. Sometimes, late at night, he would sneak in to see her. He whispered to her as she slept. In a matter of months, he was joined on the rooftop by two others.

Mr. Gryphus was drawn upwards when the final stages of transformation were complete. Eagle-eyed, he opened his window, scaled the building and came beak to beak with Mr. Harlow. He skulked on the roof for a day and then took flight, desiring a nest of his own. Mr. Pava was second to arrive. He strutted on the ledge of the building, unsure of his next move. Mr. Harlow gave him a merciless push. It was all he needed to soar towards the cityscape where rooftops were plentiful.

Alone, Mr. Harlow stalked the courtyard when the light faded each night. An unfortunate rat was often his main source of food. That is, until he saw the little girl left behind in the dark. Too tempting for a creature such as himself, it was survival after all. Smaller birds made the tastiest dishes. The little boy from floor five was next. It was a meal satisfying enough to last several weeks.

With each bone picked clean, piled in the corner, he moved farther away from his humanity. There was only one thing that made his heart pierce with pain. He longed for Maggie. The boy from floor seven visited her often. He watched them from the massive elm tree in the courtyard. One night he noticed a rustle of feathers discreetly tucked under her shirt. His heart leapt with joy, Maggie would soon be joining him. The days wore on but the final transformation didn't occur. She had always been a stubborn creature.

Restless, tired of waiting for his mate, he stole into the apartment. But she was not what he'd expected. Asleep in the nest bed, he noticed her feathers were a combination of white, black and vibrant blue.

A predator she wasn't. What nature desired for him would be impossible for her to survive. He could see it in her all too human face; as the attachment in his heart lessened, Maggie would eventually become prey. Then the boy came. A typical magpie, pocket filled with loot. The first child to undergo the evolution, he reminded Mr. Harlow of himself. He wondered if the boy had changed later, would he have manifested into a hawk? Regardless, destiny or nature had chosen magpie curiosity for the boy over cunning observation.

There was only one thing left to do. Give a lasting love token to Maggie, before retreating into the wild. Better than a diamond ring, he would leave her the terrarium nest. He would let the winged boy live. Maybe, if he could hold on a bit longer, he would check on them from afar. Make sure the night birds were keeping a distance. Anchor the furniture nest so no curious crows dared to pass. Maggie looked at him and knew what he was thinking. Silence had always been their secret language. She put her head on his chest; let his arms and wings enfold her, one last time. The hawk and the sparrow entwined, an improbable union of hearts.

Jasper woke after three moons passed. The fever had vanished leaving two, fully grown, black and white wings in its place. He sat up, scanning the glass house. The bones were gone. With no trace of grim remains, he wondered if he'd imagined them. His blue eye spotted Mrs. Harlow, morning sun filtering down on her as she stood near the ledge. It was early, the roosters crowed, but the building was still sleeping.

She was wearing a shirt dress; it had two slits cut in the back to free her pointed blue and white wings. He noticed the same had been done to his favorite shirt. With a flutter of excitement, he moved his shoulder muscles and felt the wings respond. A quick flap of the left wing. An awkward flap of the right. For the first time in his young life, Jasper felt giddy. His spied his coat draped over a lone chair. Scrambling off the suspended bed, he checked the pocket, relieved to find his treasure tin still inside.

Mrs. Harlow spotted Jasper and waved him over. He ran the length of the glass house, energy restored. With a quick kick-step, he tried to fly with no luck. Intuitively, he knew it was only a matter of time before he would glide. Jasper emerged onto the ledge next to Mrs. Harlow. There was no sign of the man-bird.

"Is the man-bird here?" he whispered.

"No, he's gone." Mrs. Harlow said, a tear twinkling in her eye.

"Was the man-bird Mr. Harlow?" Jasper asked. He wanted to make sure he understood things. Sometimes he thought he knew what he was seeing but found he was tragically mistaken. With Mrs. Harlow, he wanted lucidity.

"It was, but he's something different now," she said, wings moving nervously.

"Will we grow beaks too?" He had far too many questions that needed answering. Why did they have wings now? Was everyone going to change? Why were his wings different from Mrs. Harlow's? What happened to the pile of children bones? All of these things swirled in his mind, building unsustainable momentum by the second.

"I don't know," she answered, "but I have a feeling if we hold on to the little things, we might be able to stay as we are for a bit longer." Jasper knew that was something he was good at. His mind calmed slightly at the prospect of regaining control.

"Mrs. Harlow, am I going to live here with you now?" he asked, hoping with every fiber of his winged soul that the glass house was his new nest.

"Yes," she smiled at him. "We'll see if others start to join us." A slight twinge of fear creased her cheek but she quickly hid it, as not to worry the boy. Not all birds were sparrows or magpies. Not all people held tight to their humanity, especially when survival was at stake.

"Mrs. Harlow," Jasper said tentatively, he wanted to ask her about the bones but then changed his mind. "What will we eat?" She smiled and took his small hand in her own.

"I think we should work on bringing the terrarium back to life," she said leading Jasper back inside the glass house. He liked the idea of moths and grasshoppers dancing around a lush garden. It would be a delicatessen of insect snacks.

"Sometimes I need to count my treasures," he said nervously, hoping she would not throw his tin from the roof.

"I think you should," she whispered conspiratorially. "Maybe we can grow lucky clovers." Jasper remembered the clover on the white plate. Lucky, he thought, like number seven. He nodded excitedly, dashing forward with a slightly more successful step-kick-fly combination.

"And Jasper," Mrs. Harlow cried after him as he ran towards the terrarium. "You can call me Maggie."

Jasper imagined tucking her name into his treasure tin. His heart unencumbered by gloom, he took another leap. Wings flapping in synch, eyes closed in concentration, he remained aloft. His mind slowed to a calm hum. He rushed back to his jacket in this manner, hopeful Maggie might know how to fix the lid of his treasure box. Jasper lifted the tin between two pinched fingers. His talismans were slightly mangled and incomplete. He thought of the man-bird watching him from the roof. A slight shiver ran through his body remembering the abandoned bones. Maggie noticed Jasper shudder; she quietly divined the boy's somber musings.

"Mr. Harlow asked me to give this to you." She reached into her pocket, retrieving the lost white feather. Jasper cradled it in his hands, the abandoned plume restored. A ray of light filled his chest with unabashed joy. The little things were falling perfectly into order. All the clockworks were wound, spinning cogs ignited; Jasper knew the evolutionarium was well underway.

ACKNOWLEDGEMENTS

As always, I want to give my many thanks to all who take the time to read my stories. To my husband, Laurent Gallego, for aiding me tirelessly in combining the elements of my art into a tidy little book. To Nona Wong for your encouragement and support. Your enthusiasm for my stories makes me want to strive ahead into new imaginary realms. To Jennifer Jahahn for weeding and plucking text when necessary. Your friendship and love of words are a blessing. To Wendy Moss Thomas for being a true and enduring friend. You always inspire me to create. And to the dream world for giving me an imaginative spark for this series.

Made in the USA
Charleston, SC
13 May 2014